T0363604

## WAARDA
### SERIES FOR YOUNG READERS
Edited by Sally Morgan

a research initiative between
Fremantle Press
and
School of Indigenous Studies,
University of Western Australia

*For my Uncle Malcolm who was taken from us too early.*

# A Cyclone is Coming!

**DARLENE OXENHAM**

FREMANTLE PRESS

fine independent publishing

# Chapter One
# Pop's Water Truck

I wake with a fright to the sound of
Patches barking madly outside my
window. I pull the curtains back, open
the window and look outside. Sure
enough, Patches is right under my
window looking up at me. I smile down
at him and say, 'Okay, okay. I will take
you for a walk.' He wags his tail at me
as if to say, 'Hurry up, Annie. I have
been waiting forever.'

I live with my parents in a caravan in a place called Useless Loop and I just love it. My grandparents and their youngest children — my aunt and uncles — live next to us on the bottom terrace. It may seem a bit strange to some people but my aunty and two of my uncles are only a couple of years older than me. I don't know how this has worked out, but I am really happy that it has because they are not only my relatives but they are great friends and fun to be around.

There are only about ten other kids my age in Useless Loop and we are all friends. During the holidays we do everything together. We go swimming at the beach. We go fishing off the jetty and collecting shells. We do lots of things!

But today I have a plan. Today I am going to visit my grandad who is in charge of carting the water that we all use for drinking and cooking. It is a lovely warm sunny day and best of all it is school holidays, so I can do what I want.

'Come on, boy, let's go see Pop.'

'Woof,' replies Patches.

We walk up the caravan park terraces, looking at everything that is going on. Seagulls swoop in searching for scraps of food. Lizards scurry here and there on lizard business. Patches tries to chase a few but they always get away by running under rocks.

In the distance I can see dust on the

road out of town. That means Pop is
on his way back with a load of water.
You can always tell when Pop is coming
because of the cloud of dust stirred up
by his truck.

We wait as Pop pulls in and swings
the big hose over the top of the tank.

'Hello there little one, how are you
today?' asks Pop.

'Good, Pop. We brought you an
apple.'

'I am always pleased to see you, Bub, but I am especially pleased to see you when you have brought a snack for me.'

Pop releases a lever that pumps the water from the truck into the big water tank. As the water is pumping we sit and eat our apples.

'I'm thinking of going to the beach today, Pop,' I say.

Pop looks at the sky and then at the sea and says, 'I don't think you should. The sea looks a bit rough and the wind is getting up. Besides, your mum and dad will need your help to prepare.'

'Prepare for what?' I ask.

'The cyclone,' Pop replies. 'A cyclone is coming.'

# Chapter Two
# Preparing for the Cyclone

Well, Pop was right! Yesterday afternoon the wind started blowing and has not stopped blowing since. I have never been in a cyclone before. In fact, I'm not even sure what a cyclone really is.

'A cyclone is like a very big storm,' Dad explains. 'There is plenty of rain

and the wind can blow hundreds of
kilometres per hour and do lots and
lots of damage.'

'Oh, that sounds scary, Dad!' I say.

Dad smiles. 'It can be a bit scary,
but we need to think of it as an
adventure and be prepared. For a start,
I will go and pick up the scraper.'

'Why?' I ask.

'Because I am going to tie the caravan to it. The cyclone that's coming is pretty big — big enough to overturn a caravan. I need to tie it to something so heavy it can't move. I guarantee the caravan won't blow away if it is tied to the scraper.'

'That's for sure, Dad!'

'Come on, Annie, you can help me pick up any loose things like toys, brooms and bikes,' Mum says. 'We need to put everything away so the wind doesn't blow it into our caravan or anyone else's. After that, we need to tape up the windows.'

'Why?' I ask.

'The glass may break in the cyclone,' explains Mum. 'It depends

on how strong the winds are, but it's safer if we tape them. That way even if they do get broken they won't shatter into small pieces. The tape will hold them together. We need to leave the windows open a bit too, so that the pressure inside the caravan will be the same as it is outside.'

Wow, this is an adventure — scary but exciting!

While Dad is gone I walk over to Nan's caravan to see if they are preparing for the cyclone as well. As I step through the door I can hear Nan in the kitchen of the caravan, and I see my aunty — Joyce — and two uncles — Neville and Malcolm — playing cards at the table in the annexe.

Nan pops her head out of the caravan and calls, 'Hey sweetie, have you come for a visit?'

'I'm waiting for Dad to come back with the scraper and thought I would come and see what you were doing,' I reply.

'Well,' Nan says, 'I was just trying to get those lazybones,' she gestures to my aunt and uncles, 'to start cleaning up around here.'

I look over to where Joyce, Neville and Malcolm are playing cards and say, 'Come on then, I will help you until Dad gets back.'

As we are finishing the cleaning around Nan's caravan, I hear Dad call out, 'Do you want to help me tie down the caravan, Annie? All you have to do is catch the rope when I throw it to you.' I race back home to help.

In the end I have to catch three ropes. Each of the ropes is tied to a plastic-covered chain that Dad drags across the caravan and then ties securely to the scraper. There is no way our caravan is going to blow away!

# Chapter Three
## Waiting for the Cyclone

We have tidied up everything. All my toys are stacked away. Nothing loose has been left lying around. All the cleaning has been done. I don't think there is anything else to do.

'Last-minute check,' Mum calls to Dad.

'Spare batteries for the radio,' she says.

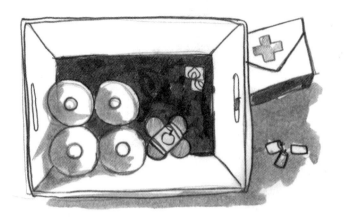

'Check,' answers Dad.

'Full water containers.'

'Check.'

'Canned food.'

'Check.'

'Ice for esky and frozen food moved.'

'Check.'

'Matches and gas bottles.'

'Check.'

'Portable stove.'

'Check.'

'Sleeping bags.'

'Check.'

'First aid kit.'

'Check.'

So we have done everything that we need to do. Now all that's left is to wait for the cyclone to hit.

# Chapter Four
## The Countdown

Waiting for a cyclone is a scary time
AND a boring time.

After lunch Mum, Dad and I play
board games in our annexe. We have
played one game of Monopoly and just
finished Snakes and Ladders. I lost!

'When is the cyclone meant to get
here, Dad?' I ask.

'The last radio broadcast estimated
the cyclone would hit us late in the

afternoon,' Dad replies.

I look at the clock and groan. It is only one o'clock so it could be hours before the cyclone gets here.

Mum puts my *Harry Potter and the Goblet of Fire* DVD on. This is my favourite Harry Potter movie and I must have watched it about ten times now. The movie is halfway through when suddenly the power goes off.

'Oh my god,' I yell. 'Does this mean the cyclone is here now?'

'Shh, be calm,' Dad says. 'The cyclone is not here yet. The power has been turned off as a safety measure.'

My heart is still pumping hard as I stand in the middle of our small kitchen, not really sure what to do with myself.

Mum reaches for my hand and says,
'Come and help me put out the torches
and lamps ready for when it gets dark.'

Dad turns up the radio to listen to
the cyclone update.

'Residents of Denham and Useless
Loop are warned that Cyclone Tessie is

approximately two hours away. Cyclone Tessie is a category 3 cyclone with expected wind gusts of 150 kilometres per hour. Residents are urged to stay inside at all times and to ensure that loose materials are secured. Regular cyclone updates will be broadcast each hour.'

'Right. We need to do the final jobs now,' says Dad.

'But I thought that we had done them all,' I say.

'Not quite,' replies Dad.

# Chapter Five
# Our Safe Place

In a cyclone everyone is told to identify the safest place in the home. Our safe place turns out to be the kitchen of our caravan. Dad explains that this is the safest place for us because we are protected by the seats along the wall of the caravan and by the kitchen cuboards, so we have a barrier between us and any stuff flying into the caravan.

Dad has put three mattresses

on the kitchen floor and folded the table down and put a big double bed mattress on top as another layer of protection.

'If I tell you to hide, you have to quickly squeeze yourself under the kitchen table and stay there until Mum or I tell you that you can move,' Dad says.

This scares me a lot because there is only space for me under the table. I wonder what will happen to Mum and Dad but I don't say anything. I just nod.

I look at the clock on the wall.

'Dad, Mum, look — it's half past three. The cyclone will be here soon!'

I walk over to the window and look outside. In the sky I can see dark clouds gathering to block out the sun. It smells of rain.

Patches has made himself a nice little bed under the kitchen table and looks like he is settled in for the night. We spread out our sleeping bags and pillows and get comfortable. I hear the rain begin to fall lightly on the caravan.

Dad opens up a special box he has packed. In the box is my portable DVD player and several movies; there are five bottles of water, candles, matches, some tins of tuna and other food, books, comics and crosswords, a deck of cards and other games.

'See — everything we need to weather a cyclone,' Dad says.

Mum opens her book and begins to read as Dad and I start our first game of cards. Outside the sky is darker and the rain is heavier. The wind has started to really blow. I can hear the annexe whipping backwards and forwards as the wind gusts push it in and out. The rain beats down hard on the caravan. Thud, thud, thud, thud, thud. It is getting scary now. Dad has to turn up the radio to hear what is being said.

'We interrupt this program with a news update. Cyclone Tessie is now passing over the townships of Denham

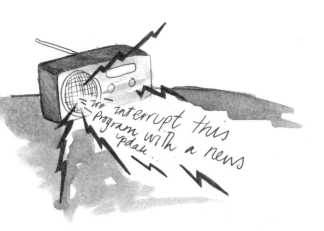

and Useless Loop. Wind gusts have
been recorded at 156 kilometres per
hour. The cyclone is approximately 100
kilometres wide. Residents of Denham
and Useless Loop are advised not to
venture outside — that is, under no
circumstances go outside. The cyclone
is expected to take six hours to pass
over Denham and Useless Loop.'

# Chapter Six
# The Cyclone Is Here!

Mum looks at me and sees how scared I am.

'Come and jump into bed next to me,' she says, 'We can read a comic together.'

Outside the wind is howling around the caravan. The annexe is flapping so much I worry the stakes will never hold.

'It is okay. Everything will be fine,' reassures Dad.

I look at the clock. This is going to go on for hours, I think in despair. I try to concentrate on my *Superman* comic, but after reading the same page five times I give up. I can't concentrate at all.

'Righto, everyone. I think we should have an early dinner,' announces Mum.

We have chicken and corn soup which Dad heats up on the small gas

burner, followed by tuna and salad sandwiches, then tinned peaches and ice-cream from the esky.

Patches pops his head out from under the table to get his dinner and then goes right back and immediately off to sleep. I wish I could do the same!

While we eat, the wind and rain get

heavier and louder outside.

After dinner Dad suggests that I watch another movie with my headphones on. This is not so bad because all I can hear is the movie. As I watch I glance over at Mum and Dad several times. They have their heads together talking, but they don't look really worried.

If they are not worrying, I think, then I won't either. And I don't, until the movie finishes and I take my headphones off. The noise is incredible. The caravan is beginning to sway and shudder.

Dad looks at me and says, 'Don't be afraid. We are not going to blow away. Remember, we are tied to a twenty-tonne scraper. Not even this wind can drag us away from that. Choose another movie.'

Halfway through *Transformers*, Dad taps me on the shoulder and gestures for me to take the headphones off. When I do, all I can hear is … silence. No wind, no rain; and it is sunny! I cannot believe it. Dad takes me to the window so I can look outside. It is amazing. It is just like a nice normal day.

'This is the eye of the cyclone. Incredible, isn't it,' Dad says. 'The eye is at the centre of the cyclone and it is very calm — no wind, no rain. But you must not be fooled, because once this passes then the winds and rain are back again. So you must never go outside when the eye of the cyclone is passing.'

Dad and I watch until the sky begins to darken, a light rain starts falling and the wind gusts get stronger again. Soon the wind is once again howling and the rain pounding down on the caravan. The caravan is shaking so much it begins to make squeaking noises. It is like a giant hand is pushing against it.

I lie next to Mum again to read my comic. Mum is reading her book and Dad is doing a crossword and listening to the radio. This has been a very scary and exhausting day but there is no way I will be able to sleep tonight.

What will tomorrow bring?

# Chapter Seven
# After The Storm

We are all up early in the morning. I really didn't think I would sleep last night, but I did. I think that in a strange way the swaying of the caravan actually helped me sleep!

Patches is desperate to go to the toilet and we want to see what damage the cyclone has done.

The first thing I notice when we walk outside is all the broken branches

and leaves. They are everywhere. There is no wind or rain but the ground is very muddy.

We walk around our caravan and annexe but everything is fine and in its place.

'See — the scraper was a good idea, wasn't it,' Dad says.

'Sure was, Dad!' I reply.

We walk over to Nan and Pop's to make sure that everything is okay at their place. Nan and Pop, and Joyce, Neville and Malcolm, join us outside, and we stand together looking at all the other caravans. Suddenly Malcolm points and yells, 'Look at that!' We look in the direction he is pointing and see a dinghy leaned up against a caravan.

'Must have been blown off its trailer,' Pop observes.

'Hey, I wonder what else has been blown around,' says Joyce.

'Dad, can we go and have a look?' I plead.

Dad looks at Pop before he replies, and Pop nods his consent.

'Yes, you can. But stay together and be careful,' Dad instructs.

We all take off at a run. We wander around for about an hour looking at all the things that had been blown about. Some people had forgotten about

their bins and these had been blown
over and all the rubbish thrown out.
I see four seagulls land and begin to
scavenge through the rubbish looking
for juicy bits to eat.

Everyone in Useless Loop is out and
looking at the damage caused by the
cyclone.

'I think we have been lucky,' says
Neville. 'Really there is not much
damage and no one got hurt.'

Neville is right. It looks like one huge mess, but really it won't take too long to clean it all up. We are lucky. It's strange how last night I was so very scared and now today I feel excited. Everything is okay and it is a new day with new adventures to come.

# Chapter Eight
# Back To School

'Who wants to tell news?' asks Mrs Frost, our teacher.

I slowly put my hand up.

'Annie, good. Thank you for being first,' says Mrs Frost.

'My news today is about the cyclone,' I begin. I hear a few groans around the class and someone whispers, 'Boring.'

I continue, ignoring the comments

of my very rude friends.

'After the cyclone Joyce, Neville, Malcolm and I looked all over the caravan park to see what damage had been done. Then Malcolm said why don't we go to the beach and so we did and there were lots of things that we found.'

I look at my aunt and uncles for help and Malcolm starts wiggling and shaking his arms around.

'Is there something you would like to share, Malcolm?' asks Mrs Frost.

'Yes. We found an octopus,' says Malcolm. He takes out a glass jar and puts it on his desk. The kids rush over to look at the octopus.

'Everyone, back to your own seats NOW!' says Mrs Frost sternly. 'Annie, as you found these things with Neville, Malcolm and Joyce, they can also tell news with you. Go ahead.'

'We found a crab that had died,' I say. This time Neville brings out a square tin container. He opens the lid to reveal a greenie-blue crab with a few missing legs.

'Children, stay where you are,' instructs Mrs Frost before anyone can get up. 'Neville, pass it around so everyone can have a look.'

'We also found a

flat tyre tube, a broken kite and a dead stingray which we didn't bring because it smelt bad,' I say, screwing up my nose as I remember it.

'But the best thing we found was a bottle.' I look at Joyce who is holding up a light-green bottle. 'It had a cork in the top and a message inside.'

Everyone is very excited.

'Did you read the message?'

'What did it say?'

'Who was it from?'

I look at Neville, Malcolm and Joyce and we all smile.

'Yes, we read the message,' I say. 'But *that* is another story,' I finish smugly and sit down.

There is silence.

'Have you finished telling your news now?' asks Mrs Frost curiously.

'Yes,' replies Neville.

'Ah, a mystery,' says Mrs Frost. 'Well, Tom, perhaps you would like to go next and tell us about how your annexe fell down?'

Everyone groans as Tom stands to tell his news about the cyclone.

# About the Author

My name is Darlene Oxenham. I was born in Denham, Shark Bay. I am a Malgana woman. My country is around Shark Bay, between Geraldton and Carnarvon on the coast of Western Australia.

My story was inspired by our time living in Useless Loop and is written with thanks to my parents who looked after us through many cyclones and floods, and who provided valuable advice on this book.

I want to give particular thanks to my grandparents, Maude and Stump, and make special mention of my aunty Joyce and uncles Neville and Malcolm whose real names I use to give them full acknowledgement. We did live next door to each other at Useless Loop and our time there was a time of innocence and wonder that I value greatly to this day.

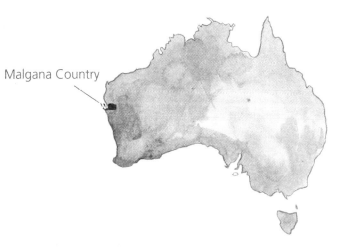

Malgana Country

FREMANTLE PRESS
25 Quarry Street, Fremantle, 6160
(PO Box 158, North Fremantle 6159)
Western Australia
www.fremantlepress.com.au

Cover Designer Allyson Crimp
Cover Artwork Sally Morgan
Internal artwork and design Tracey Gibbs (www.traceygibbs.com)
Printed by Everbest Printing Company, China.

National Library of Australia
Cataloguing-in-publication entry

Author: Oxenham, Darlene.
Title: A cyclone is coming! / Darlene Oxenham.
Edition: 1st ed.
ISBN: 9781922089342 (pbk.)
Series: Waarda ; 9.
Dewey number: A823.4

Government of **Western Australia**
Department of **Culture and the Arts**

Fremantle Press is supported by the State Government
through the Department of Culture and the Arts.